THE TENT

Kealan Patrick Burke

Copyright 2013 by Kealan Patrick Burke
Cover Design by Elderlemon Design

ISBN-13: 978-1985863781
ISBN-10: 1985863782

THE TENT

KEALAN PATRICK BURKE

1

PEPPER IS NERVOUS, and that in turn makes McCabe uneasy. The collie is not given to barking at every sound or she'd long ago have driven him insane. Up here in the mountains, they have long shared real estate with rabbits, cows, deer and sheep, and birds aplenty. Pepper learned this as a pup, learned to recognize the ambient sounds of the mountain's many residents, and now rarely does she raise her head from her tattered old wicker basket in the corner of the cabin.

Tonight, however, her head and her hackles are raised. Her brown eyes are wide and wet and fixed on the door of his small bungalow as if trouble casts its shadow on the other side.

Sitting before the fire, the air tinged with smoke, the damp logs still crackling and spitting three hours after he set them alight, McCabe watches the dog watching the door, and cocks his own head in an effort to detect whatever might have upset his old friend. Unsurprisingly, he hears nothing but the wind. Twenty years ago, maybe even ten, he'd have stood a slim chance of competing with the dog's hearing, but not anymore. They are both in the winters of their lives, but Pepper still has the edge on him when it comes to the senses.

Reluctantly he stands, his knees crackling louder than the logs, and puts one rough hand on his lower back, absently massaging away the dull fiery pain that settles in like a cuckoo whenever the weather turns cold. Pepper gives him a brief glance, her worried eyes reflecting the small flames in the hearth, clearly unwilling to break her concentration from whatever has her dander up, and goes back to watching the door.

"What is it, Pep?" he asks in a soothing voice. "What's got you upset?"

The dog whines but does not look at him.

Visitors are rare during the day, and rarer still at night. When anyone does have occasion to seek his cabin out, it is seldom with good news.

As he shrugs on his peacoat and sighs, Pepper gingerly steps from her basket and plods over to join him. She trembles slightly and McCabe doesn't like that at all. She may be old, but he has always thought of her as fearless. He reaches down and he is alarmed when the dog lowers her head as if afraid she is about to be struck, something he has never done in all their years together.

He frowns. "This is one of those times I wish you could talk," he says, something he has wished often in the four years since his wife Susan passed away.

Coat fastened, he fetches his old hand-carved, bleached pine walking stick from the corner by the door and turns his attention back to the dog.

Her head is still bowed in deference to the unknown threat. As he watches her tremble, he briefly considers abandoning the idea of venturing out into the cold and giving Trooper Lyons a call instead. Then he just as quickly dismisses the notion. Lyons is a good and fair man, but he's also a drunk and as it's after ten on a Wednesday night, the chances of finding him sober are slim. He'd undoubtedly balk at the idea of the twenty-mile drive to the mountain, especially to investigate what will no doubt prove to be little more than the result of a nervous dog's hypersensitivity. Instead he'll slur a few reassurances and promise to stop by in the morning. But because McCabe has unwavering faith in his dog's ability to sense something amiss out there, he doesn't fancy the idea of waiting that long. The wondering will keep him awake all night if he doesn't go see what it is.

"How likely am I to run into a demon or a ghost out there, girl?" he asks the dog.

Pepper says nothing, just looks through him to the door as if, merely by mentioning it, he has become a ghost himself.

And though the old man feels silly at the note of fear pealing through him, he can't deny that the dog has him more worried than he's accustomed to being. The last time he saw Pepper this alarmed, McCabe had stood up from the supper table and followed her outside into the fine spring evening, where he found his wife lying prostrate in the yard, her heart as dead and cold as the rocks upon which she lay, her laundry basket turned on its side, the freshly laundered clothes strewn about her head and shoulders.

He doesn't like to think about that now, no more than he likes the waves of terror that radiate from the dog and creep into the marrow of his old bones.

Something is wrong out there, and he tells himself that if he has any sense at all, he'll stay locked up inside with the old girl and wait until sunup to go investigate. But then he reminds himself that people sometimes get themselves in trouble on the mountain; youngsters mostly, sometimes the occasional hiker who tries to scale the peak without doing their homework first. The mountainside is full of bottomless holes and crevasses partially concealed by shrubbery, mires disguised as weed-choked clearings, and loose shale that can go from under you in a heartbeat and send you tumbling. He's watched many a man being airlifted off the slope, fielded questions about youths gone missing, some of whom showed up looking worse for wear, some of whom were never seen again. And every time he'd felt a twinge of guilt for not intervening, for not shooing them off the slope or at least giving them some advice on how best to proceed if they were determined to carry on. He knows it is ridiculous, of course. He can hardly be held responsible for what others choose to do of their own free will, but the fact of the matter is that nobody out here knows the mountain better than he does—he has after all, lived here for the greater part of his long life—and so he feels a sort of guardianship toward both the mountain and the people who traverse its hostile terrain. He is one of the few people who still call the mountain home, the lure of the big city too great to resist and the increasing lack of agricultural viability too great to survive. He knows the mountain is a dangerous place, but he has never really feared it, despite acknowledging that there are things about it that he can't explain and that don't always make sense.

But thanks to Pepper, he fears it now.

"C'mon then," he tells the dog, and tries not to let her anxiety freeze him in place. With one last longing look back at the fire, he sighs, snatches a flashlight from its hook by the door, and opens the door to the night.

It is quiet out there. No birdsong, no bark of mating animals, no shriek of cornered prey. The slope rises greenly up to his left until swathed by a dark bandolier of beech and oak. Boulders speckle the plain around his small cabin, looking like knuckled bones in the cloudy moonlight.

Behind him, Pepper whines on the threshold, the small silver bell on her collar jingling as she reluctantly does her duty and follows her master out the door.

Troubled, he closes the door behind her, offers her a soothing word she does not, despite the acuity of her senses, seem to hear, and heads off toward the only thing on the mountain that has immediately registered as out of place: the small amber glow of a campsite somewhere up there in the trees. He assumes that if there's something amiss, he'll find it there. What he does not yet know is the nature of the trouble, and offers up a silent prayer to his deceased wife that he will not regret answering its call.

2

THE STORM HAD COME UPON THEM without warning, a hungry, violent thing that roared in from the north, as if they'd camped on a railroad track assumed abandoned only to have a freight train barrel through in an explosion of sudden light and noise.

And now their tent was destroyed, and they were lost in the dark woods, having fled in the kind of panic unique to unseasoned campers, shelter taking precedence over direction.

"Mike? Do you know where we're going?"

"Sure, babe."

This is the first of many lies he has told her on this trip, and he fears it won't be the last. They're lost, and it's his fault—of course it is, isn't everything?—but Mike is determined not to acknowledge the fact if only to deprive his wife of just one more reason to think less of him.

"You're sure?" Emma yells at him over the wind and rain that sends spectral horses galloping through his flashlight beam.

The verdure weaves and dances around them in submarine symphony. They are miles from anywhere. There are only trees here, tall and stolid and dark, the forest floor soft and spongy, greedily sucking down the rain and their ill-prepared feet after months of drought. Above their heads, the canopies of the beech, poplar, and oak are thick enough to appear conjoined, relegating the lightning to startlingly bright pulses between the crowded boles.

Mike stops, eager to go on, eager to be out of this interminable forest, but glad for the chance to catch his breath, which a quarter mile or so ago became labored and now feels like he's pulling flaming cotton into his lungs instead of air. The hiking boots he bought just for this occasion are sawing open the backs of his heels, making each step torture. He turns to face his wife and son, knowing they need reassurance, knowing he could use it just as much, and struggles against the encumbrance of the backpack full of items that were of little enough use before the storm and are useless now, and his yellow slicker, which flaps madly as if eager to free of him. He empathizes, eager as he is right now to be free of himself and the situation into which he has thrust them. This was a mistake, and probably the last one he'll ever make as a married man. That it was supposed to revitalize their crumbling union is only the larger part of the tragedy this trip has become. That he knew his luck would pull the rug out from under him is another. Because the last time he can remember his poor luck changing to any substantial degree, he was three weeks shy of his thirty-first birthday, still living with his parents, unemployed and flirting with alcoholism as a way to subvert his loneliness, when he answered the door to a perky blonde, her pretty face glowing with rehearsed Republican charm as she espoused the benefits of reelecting George Bush Sr. It had taken uncharacteristic levels of courage and impulsivity for him to ask out a girl he knew was so far out of his league they likely didn't share the same quality of oxygen, but it had to have been pure luck, or some other strange upset in the mechanics of the universe, that had made her response an affirmative one. Luckier still that he hadn't blown it on their subsequent dates, that she hadn't seen—or that she chose to ignore—the insecurity that hounded him like a starving dog he'd been foolish enough to feed and now couldn't shake.

That blonde is not as pretty now, and he knows not all of that can be blamed on the weather. Her red slicker clings to a body made shapeless by the years, the disappointment, and the stress of being married to a man crippled by the ever-increasing weight of his own failure and unrealized dreams. Her hair, which has lost its luster and faded in synch with her expectations of him, is pasted to her pallid face, but not enough to hide the doubt from eyes made darker by the shadow of his presence in their marriage.

"I think so, yes," he tells her, and even to his own ears it sounds like a "no". But the lies seem to come easier the deeper into the woods they go, and he doesn't care if they've become as transparent as the rain-horses riding through their flashlight beams. He can see on her face and in her posture as she hugs herself against the relentless battering of the storm that she recognizes the lie, but knows better than to challenge it, especially when she is not the only one who might suffer from its exposure. With a smile of feeble wattage, she turns away from him and drops to her knees on the sodden, steaming carpet of dead leaves. Cody, their thirteen-year-old, who has been trailing them soundlessly and with a complete and enviable absence of worry, finds her face with his flashlight beam.

The boy smiles, and as he looks from his mother's face to the storm-wracked woods around them, Mike sees the twin sparks of wonder in his son's eyes, and feels a tightening in his throat. The boy has a spirit he could not possibly have inherited from his parents, the genesis of his cheerful disposition an equal mystery. Tears prick the corners of Mike's own eyes and he does not bother to sleeve them away. The rain will excuse them.

I don't want to lose my son, he thinks.

Whatever Emma is saying to the boy is lost in a peal of thunder that sounds like the roar of some forest god enraged by their intrusion, and even as Mike winces against the violence of it, he tries to read in Cody's face the impact of Emma's words.

I don't want to lose my boy, he thinks, *don't take him from me.* The dread that lies like a cold hard stone in the pit of his belly is a wicked thing, an ever-present thing, and with it comes an irrational certainty that whatever his wife is saying, it is designed to undermine the child's confidence in his father's ability to see them through this nightmare.

Worse, he knows such speculation may be depressingly close to the mark.

It's time we had a talk about Daddy, he imagines his wife telling their child. *It's time for you to realize the sad truths we've been keeping from you. First of all, we're lost because your father thought taking us into the wilderness would somehow keep us together. But it won't, because I hate him, and in time, you'll learn to hate him too. But don't worry; I plan to get us both away before he can destroy your life like he did Mommy's. That is, if we don't die out here first.*

Cody picks that moment to nod in agreement, compounding Mike's paranoia, and abruptly he is reminded of his own childhood, specifically his mother's habit of turning the volume on the TV down to nothing whenever a character started using foul language, like "damn" or "heck", or discussing subjects she deemed inappropriate, like alcohol, or drugs, or romance. *Not for your ears, Mikey*, she would tell him, and he would wait impatiently for the sound to come back. Sometimes the silence only lasted until the scene changed, or until the commercials. Sometimes his mother would get distracted and forget to turn it back up at all, and he would be sent to bed with a headful of questions about what those characters might have been discussing that was so terrible he'd been forbidden from hearing it. He would learn it all in the schoolyard when the other kids discussed the latest episodes of *Hawaii Five-0* and *Bonanza*, and he would laugh right along, pretending he was one of them, knowing he wasn't. Since then, he has been an outsider, and he is made intrinsically aware of that feeling again now as he stands watching his wife counseling his son in a dire situation of Mike's own making, helpless to do anything but hope he's wrong about the weight of their words.

As the thunder rolls away into the woods to the left of them, Emma touches the boy's cheek and rises. As she approaches Mike, she folds her arms again—a natural reaction to the hostile weather, but also, according to their marriage counselor, a defensive posture, the manifestation of which seems directly proportional to her proximity to her husband. When she reaches him, he sees that she is shivering.

"Is it safe to be out here with all this lightning?"

"It's not like we have a choice," he says. "But we'll be fine."

"Well, whatever the case, we should keep going," she says, a bead of rain suspended from a nose the cold has made red and raw.

He nods. "I think we should be close to the campground offices. Can't be more than ten, twenty minutes from here."

She looks at him for a long moment before speaking again. "What makes you think that?"

It's a question he had hoped she wouldn't ask, because the truth is that he *doesn't* think that, has no idea how far they are from anything except lost. The truth is that he knew an hour ago, right around the time he felt the ground begin to rise ever so slightly upward instead of down, that they had gotten completely turned around. The campground offices were in a small valley between the hills. This much, he remembered. If they were headed the right way, the going would have been easier because they'd have been on a decline. The trees would have thinned out too, but the longer they walk, the denser the woods become. The reality, as terrible as it is, is that, yes, he has them well and truly lost, probably miles away from anyone who might be able to help, and all he's doing now is walking in the hope of finding a cabin, or a lodge, or any kind of shelter.

He knows Emma knows this too, and that the long look she gave him was her way of parting the veil of his deception and looking at the complete truth of the matter for herself. He decides the best thing to do is to change the subject, and what better subject than the one that's hanging over them as heavy as the storm.

"About earlier..." he says.

She shrugs, but does not meet his gaze. "Forget it. You were upset."

"Yeah, but still, I shouldn't have snapped at you. It wasn't your fault. The tent was a cheap piece of crap anyway."

The slight smile is very slight indeed, but more than he hoped for, so it will do just fine for now. "Yeah, it was. I did try to tell you that. Made a better kite than a tent."

The levity, here in this frightening, storm-washed darkness, is so unexpected and so desperately needed, he bursts out laughing. Cody, still enthralled by the hissing, weaving, thunderous woods around them, looks in their direction and smiles. *Such a happy child*, he thinks. *So unflappable. He didn't get that from me.* But in the extensive catalogue of his failures, he's thankful that he can at least count his son as a success, a good thing, the one bright spot in the Rorschach pattern of his uneven life, even if, ultimately, he cannot find a way to keep them all together.

And yet you didn't want him here. This is yet another unpleasant truth. It isn't that he doesn't love the boy, because he does, more than anything. It was just that he'd wanted to be alone with Emma, to get her out of the quagmire of routine of which their son was an integral part, and to discuss with her the kinds of pressing issues not meant to be spoken aloud around children for fear of shattering their illusion of familial security. That she had insisted on bringing Cody with them gave the impression that she wasn't nearly as enthused at the idea of being alone with him as he'd been. Even his choice of destination had left her nonplussed.

"If you want to take a trip, why don't we go to a resort somewhere and enjoy a little luxury for a while?" she'd said, and even now he can't say why that had rankled so much. Perhaps it was the implication that she had *never* enjoyed luxury with him and would have embraced the opportunity to do so. Either way, it has been a disaster from the start, and nothing that's happened since has improved the quality of the situation. Until now.

Emma's smile has grown, just a bit, but these days that might as well be a brilliant lighthouse beam in the dark, scalding away the shadows, at least for a little while. It gives him hope, however tenuous, that maybe things *can* get better.

"It sure did fly, didn't it?" he says, and pictures their miserable old tent, picked up from the clearance section at their local Wal-Mart for a song. Less than five minutes into the storm, and with the sound of staggered applause, the wind tore it free of the pegs and sent it flying away like a pterodactyl to tangle itself high in the canopy above their heads, where it flapped and twisted and snapped like a creature chastising them for trying to keep it tethered. In retrospect, the image was comical, but at the time, exposed to the sudden shock of the cold rain and biting wind, and yet another goddamn disaster in a year, a *life*, replete with them, his initial reaction had been to blame Emma for not hammering the pegs in deep enough. If he was honest, he still believed that, but if accountability was the game du jour, then he'd already beaten her by a wide margin. She might have lost the tent; he had gotten *them* lost. And considering his fears about the fragility of their marriage, it had been foolish to rebuke her for anything at all.

"Have you checked your phone?" she asks.

"Yeah. I've been keeping it off to save the battery, but I checked it about ten minutes ago. Still no signal. That was kind of the point of coming here, but it sure doesn't help us much in a pinch, does it? How about yours?"

"Left it in the car. Didn't think we'd need it."

The idea of the battered old Toyota (itself so cheap and old, it has contributed to multiple instances of Mike's bad luck) with its shelter and warmth, is like an oasis to Mike. In daylight, he figures it might even be visible from here, but at night, with the storm raging around them, he might as well have parked on the moon.

"What about that compass app thingy you downloaded for Cody?"

"It would need to know our location via the GPS," he says. "And if we had the GPS, we'd have the location, and we wouldn't be lost." As the words leave his mouth on a cloud of staggered vapor, he realizes they represent the first honest answer to the question she asked in the beginning, and his smile fades. "I'm sorry," he says, wincing as a fresh gust of wind sprays rain into their faces. "I messed up."

She chooses not to acknowledge his confession, and that is somehow worse than if she had. It suggests her expectations of him are right where he has always feared they would one day end up, and where they themselves are now: somewhere south of nowhere.

"Let's not let Cody hear that, all right? I don't want to scare him."

He nods his agreement. "I don't think we have anything to worry about there. If anything, he seems to be *enjoying* this."

"Well, you promised an adventure. Looks like he's having one."

It was supposed to be an adventure for them all. A more stable, more carefree couple might still have been able to view it as one. But stable they are not, and labeling this an adventure now would only be a form of denial.

"I still can't believe it's even possible to get lost in this day and age," she says.

"People get lost all the time."

"I know, but…" She gestures helplessly at the dark theater of their surroundings, her flashlight illuminating the sinuously moving boughs above their heads. "We didn't camp that far from the trail, did we? I mean, shouldn't it have been easier to find? How did we go so far off track?"

There is no accusation in her tone, but his conscience is a lot less forgiving. He had, in actual fact, disregarded the suggestion (warning) from the camp attendant in favor of a more out of the way (prohibited) area, a more great outdoorsy (unincorporated) place rather than the large, fenced-in patch of worn earth they would have had to share with two other couples (both of whom had had much more impressive tents and so were probably safe and dry right now). In his youth he'd gone camping with his father a few times, and those occasions were some of the best moments of his life. He had hoped in keeping with the wildness of the location, he could recreate the spirit of those cherished trips, could reproduce with his own family the bond he'd forged with his father. Back then you didn't need to book a place, or get anybody's permission. You just geared up and went hiking until you found the perfect spot to set up stakes. The real, honest-to-goodness camping experience. And if something went wrong, well, that was part of the adventure too.

But now, in place of adventure, there was only misery and panic that increased exponentially with every mile they covered.

"After the tent blew away," he admits, "I thought I was leading us back to the trail. I guess I got turned around."

"Should we try to find a shelter, maybe under one of the bigger trees? Maybe light a fire or something? We'll freeze out here."

"We're under the only kind of shelter this part of the woods offers and we're still getting soaked. Best to just keep moving for now, like you said. I'm sure we'll come across a ranger station or something sooner or later."

"A ranger station? We're in Hocking Hills, Mike, not Yellowstone. How much research did you do before you dragged us up here? You're more likely to find a moonshine still here than a ranger station."

"Hell, right now I'd settle for that." When she doesn't return his smile, he continues, "But seriously, there are a few cabins around these woods. We saw one of them on the way up here, remember? We're sure to come across one if we soldier on a bit further."

"Cabins, sure," she says, and gives a slight shake of her head, "Which begs the question why you didn't just book one of *those* instead of insisting we rough it."

And there it is. This time there was no attempt to keep the resentment from her tone. Gone is the levity, the ceasefire, the pretense that anything is going to be all right. Juliet slamming the window shut on poor old Romeo. And now he knows they have to keep moving, have to find a way out of this damn weather and this predicament, because with every hour that passes in these godforsaken woods, they are getting more and more lost, the rift he had hoped to heal widening with every step they take in the wrong direction. The storm is softening the walls of his marital house, the rain implanting mold beneath the plaster, and soon it will weaken them, force them to crumble until the whole place comes crashing down.

"Sorry," he mutters too low for her to hear over the wind that makes the trees sound as if their branches are laden with snakes. He turns and manages half a step before Emma's hand slams down on his shoulder, startling a cry from him, her nails digging into his flesh through the thin protection of his slicker. Hissing pain through his teeth, he turns and sees her face has turned white, whiter than before. She has become a ghost with coals for eyes, and fear colder than the wind, colder than the rain seizes him, just as it appears to have seized her.

"Emma, what—?"

"*Cody*," she all but screams at him, the rain streaming down her face making her look as if she's melting before him.

His confusion evaporates as he looks over her shoulder.

The boy is gone.

3

H E CAN'T HAVE GONE FAR," he tells her, struggling to keep the panic from his voice.

"Really?" She has fallen into step behind him, one hand clutched on his backpack to steady herself as she makes her treacherous way across the deadfall. It has the effect of adding her weight to his already cumbersome load. "So, finally you've gotten a handle on direction, have you?"

"God damn it, leave me alone," he mutters under his breath, then curses when his foot comes down in on a patch of ground that's not ground at all, but a water-filled hollow. Cold water seeps into his boot up to the laces. The burst blister on his heel catches fire.

Lightning flares, turning the tree trunks to stone and sending thick spears of shadow into the cobalt spaces between them, but they reveal nothing to Mike but more felled trees, scrub, and waterlogged forest floor.

As they march back the way they came, pausing every few seconds in the lulls between flares of lightning to lance with their flashlight beams the boil of the steaming dark, Mike knows it's time to give up, not on the boy, no, never that, but himself. All that matters now is finding Cody and getting them all out of here. And once he does—what then? Divorce, probably. He's tired, just as worn out as Emma, and just as sick of trying so hard for little reward. He may be naïve in certain ways, but he's far from stupid. And a man would have to be some kind of dumb not to be able to read the signals his wife has been sending him for the past eight months. She's done, and if he had any sense at all, he'd be done too. All this trying to make her change her mind about him, about *them*, has done nothing but make him appear sad and desperate, which he is, and it's exhausting, and it makes him hate himself.

Sometimes, it even makes him angry, though he's never quite sure at whom that anger is directed.

Right now, she's making it a little easier to for him to focus that anger.

He stops to wait as she clamps her flashlight between her knees, raises her hands to cup her mouth, and cries out the boy's name. He has already told her Cody won't hear her over the storm, but she's a mother, and mothers don't listen to anything but their own hearts when it comes to their children.

As he sweeps his light across the boles, fear twists his guts. They will find the boy—he knows this, has to believe they will—but this interim, the waiting until they do, is terrifying. Their attention was only away from the boy for a few minutes, so he truly believed what he had told Emma: The boy could not have gone far. Probably just snuck behind a tree to take a whizz, in which case moving further away from where they'd been was probably an even worse idea.

"Emma," he says, when she pauses to take a breath to power another cry for the boy.

She looks at him, eyes dark with anger, electric with fear. "What?"

"We shouldn't go any further."

"We have to find him. We have to find where he is."

"I know." A wild gust of wind strong enough to make him stagger drowns out his words, and he waits for it to abate. *We're doing everything wrong.* Pulling his hood tight against his face to protect himself from the needling of the icy rain, he tries again. "I know, but I figure he just went to find some privacy so he could take a leak, maybe." *Please let that be it.*

Hope reduces some of the darkness in her eyes as the idea takes hold. "So, what do we do?"

"We go back to where we were and wait there. If he comes back and we're not where he left us, we'll lose him for sure."

She nods. "Okay, but let's hurry."

He does, and together they retrace their steps for a second time. At least this time, they know where they're going. Along the way, in a stroke of luck Mike is almost afraid to acknowledge lest it reverse itself out of spite, the rain begins to ease off, the wind to lessen to a bluster, like a belligerent drunk losing steam. And by the time they reach the spot where they last saw Cody, the area memorable only because of a half-buried sandstone boulder protruding from the mud and deadfall like the shoulder-bone of a felled giant, the rain stops completely. Mike yanks down his hood and takes a deep breath, as if they have spent the past few hours not in a storm, but underwater, and leans back against the boulder, grateful for the temporary reprieve from the backpack's weight.

"So, where the hell is he?" Emma asks, and when he looks at her, he sees the anger has returned. He watches her pallor deepen as the storm clouds scatter, uncovering a three-quarter moon that somehow looks as stained and wretched as the boulder upon which he rests. Unzipping his windbreaker and shrugging off the pack, he raises a hand. "Just a second."

Her body thrums with impatience. "You're just going to sit there?"

"My feet hurt. Trust me, he'll be here. We just need to wait."

She stares at him for a moment. It only takes another one for her to be in his face.

And at last, the dam breaks.

"Wait? Trust you? Neither of those suggestions sound reasonable to me, Mike. We've been waiting for hours for you to show some sign that you're even slightly capable of getting us out of this mess, despite there being no evidence of you being able to do anything of the kind as long as we've known you."

We. Mike wonders if perhaps his earlier paranoia about what she might be saying to the boy was not so misguided, after all.

Her voice is very loud in the eerie stillness left in the wake of the storm.

"And: trust you? That's all I've ever done, Mike, is trust you, and look where it's gotten me. I gave up my job because you promised to take care of me, even though I loved being a teacher. You said 'trust you' then too. I look forward to the vacations you promise you'll get us with your bonus every year, but those vacations never happen because the fucking *bonuses* never happen. And I'm still waiting for you to take care of *me.* But instead what I get is you forever looking at me waiting for me to tell you everything's all right, that I'm happy with you, that nothing's your fault. All you want are reassurances that I still love you, that I'm happy with you, when you've never been able to provide good enough reasons for that to still be the case. You moon about looking as if you believe nobody *should* love you. And maybe you're right."

The color has returned to her face, the fury warming her from the inside out. Her breath steams in her face as she rages; her eyes glitter like elliptical shards of volcanic rock. "So here I am, a prisoner of my own cowardice, trapped in a marriage of habit, forty-seven years of age with my looks gone to shit, my weight all over the place, and I'm stuck in these goddamn woods with *you.* My son is missing, none of us even wanted to *be* here. I fucking *hate* the woods, Mike. I don't know how many times I've told you that, but because *you* like them, here we are, and now that it's gone to shit like everything else you touch, you've been looking at me with your sad eyes for hours hoping I'll take pity on you and as usual tell you it isn't your fault. Well, you want to know something, Mike? It damn well *is* your fault. *Every* time you fuck up, it's your fault, because you're a gutless piece of shit who makes life miserable for everyone because that's all you know how to do. You waste away at a job you despise, transferring calls to everyone else because—and I swear this should be your motto—"It's Not Your Department". And I hate it, Mike. I fucking *hate* the way you suck the life from me. I hate the way you mope around depending on me, and on Cody, to make you feel better about yourself, and to make for you your excuses for the way you are, and I hate...I..." Breathing hard, she shakes her head and brings her hands up to cover her face. Then she turns away from him, her body convulsing as she begins to sob.

Mike sits stunned, the wind knocked from his sails as he tries to digest what she has just said. It is as if the storm passed because she inhaled it, only to vomit it forth again into his face. Never in all their years together has he seen her lose her temper like this, at least not with him. He has seen her frustrated, irritated, morose. He has never seen her become the storm, and it leaves him confused. He opens his mouth to apologize until he realizes that's all he ever does. So instead he waits, takes a deep breath, and in time, allows some of the storm to infect him too, allows his own anger to leak into his throat, an emotion forced into being by the absolute absence of all others in the face of her attack.

"Finish what you were saying."

Still with her back to him, she asks, "What?"

"You were listing the things you hate. There was something else on that list. What was it? Was it me? Were you going to say that you hate me?"

She steps closer to the rank of poplars and beech and calls out for their son, her distress causing her voice to crack on the second syllable. Without the storm for competition, her voice carries far and clear, echoing through the trees long after she has fallen quiet. If Cody is anywhere close by at all, he will hear her.

"Were you going to say you hate me?" Mike repeats, and pushes away from the boulder. The backpack slides off the rock and crumples to the soft earth. He leaves it there and takes a step closer to his wife. A timid voice inside him, the same one that has kept him quiet, kept him characterized as weak his whole life, advises he stay silent until the smoke has cleared from this particular blaze. But he doesn't want to, not now, maybe not ever again. Incredibly, for a man unaccustomed to giving up on anyone but himself, he thinks he may have found the real reason for this seemingly ill-advised jaunt into the woods. He thinks he might have brought Emma here to find out, not if she still loves him or if there is anything left to save, but to find out if *he* still loves *her,* if he *wants* there to be something left to save. Because right at this moment, he is emboldened and reinvigorated to find that he might not, and that he might finally have the words to tell her as much.

The canopy drips fat, cold drops of rainwater down upon them. Steam from hot earth cooled by the storm rises in a lazy mist around their legs. Emma screams for Cody again, keeps her back to her husband, her shoulders tensing through her slicker at the sound of his approach. She folds her arms tightly. *Of course she does,* thinks Mike, *in keeping with frigid tradition.*

"Were you?" he asks again, drawing to a halt a few feet behind her.

"Just...just stop, Mike. Please," she says. "I shouldn't have said anything. Let's just focus on what's important. I just want to find Cody and get out of here."

As she cups her mouth again, preparing another summons for their wayward son, he grabs her by the shoulders, perhaps not hard enough to hurt, but harder than she is used to, at least. The surprise on her face is a wonderful thing. He relishes it, thinks that maybe he could get used to having her look at him that way again, because he's pretty sure the last time she looked at him with any respect, was on the day he first opened the door to her all those many years ago. But of course, she didn't know him then.

Sir, are you a registered voter in the state of Ohio? Good, then if I might have a couple of minutes of your time...?

He'd been willing to give her the rest of his life. But now, rather abruptly and terrifyingly, he is no longer sure that's still the case. Because he was not altogether surprised to hear that she has accumulated her share of misgivings over the course of their marriage, even if hearing them hurt. Such things stand to reason. But she might be surprised to learn that he has misgivings of his own, chief among them one she threw back in his own face: trust, or more specifically, the lack of it.

"Where was all of this during counseling?" he asks. "Counseling that *you* suggested, and *I* paid for. Where was all of this when it might have done some good, huh?"

She will not meet his gaze.

"If you hate me, I've probably earned it," he tells her, even as she jerks free of his grip and glares at him. "But you've never had cause to question my loyalty. Answer me that, at least: have you?"

"I'm not doing this right now," she says, and turns away from him again. It punches a hot steel rod of anger through his belly and he has to struggle to resist the urge to grab her and *force* her back around to look at him. But he knows that'll bring him dangerously close to a dark, forbidden place, one from which he will never be able to return.

"You had no problem giving me a rundown of my failures, babe," he says. "So you can at least admit to one of yours."

"I don't know what you're talking about."

That small voice again, pleading for reason: *Don't say it. Don't open this door. Not here, not now.*

He ignores it, taking no small measure of glee in not merely opening but kicking off the hinges a door which has long been locked to him, the contents of the room beyond a maddening mystery.

"Wednesday nights. Where do you go?"

And now she does turn to face him, whips down her own hood, her features twisted into a look of confusion. "What?"

"You heard me."

"Are you seriously asking me this? Now?"

"Yes. Where do you go on Wednesday nights? It's a simple question."

"I go to the book club. You know that."

"What book club?"

"What book...? You're losing it, Mike. Big time. And I'm not playing this game, whatever it is."

"Yes you are."

Her eyes flash anger again, and this time despite the confidence lent him by his own resentment and certainty of betrayal, it gives him pause, tells him that perhaps his suspicions are indeed wrong. Even if they're not, he is not sure he will ever be able to get her to admit that to him. Her constitution has always been the stronger one.

"Let me ask you where *you* think I go, Mike, since you're the one who doubts me."

Last chance, Mike. Last chance to keep your mouth shut and spare yourself the last shovel of grave dirt.

But the words are too far up his throat, too tantalizing on his tongue for him to swallow them now. "That book club stopped meeting at the library eight weeks ago. I checked."

She hesitates, then starts to answer, and he knows by the ugly mask her face has become that he is not going to like whatever she has to say, but then her head whips around and she gasps, backs away from him, her arm extending to point at the rank of trees, or something between them. "Mike."

His anger had not been easy to generate. His whole life he has avoided confrontation because he has never been adept at it. It did in fact require his wife's near-admission of her hatred of him for him to even know he was capable of such ire, and even then, it came from fear of rejection, of abandonment, of being forced to be alone yet again. But he finds now that it drains quickly in the face of whatever it is she may have seen. And with the reminder of where they are and what they are doing, shame burns his cheeks. *Jesus Christ, Mike*, he thinks. *Your son...*

"What is it?" he asks, and steps close, follows her gaze.

"There," she tells him, pointing at something between the trees, her own anger gone, replaced by fragile hope. "Do you see it?"

For a moment he doesn't, and feels his heart sinking, but then...there it is, a soft amber glow winking at them through the phalanx of trees from somewhere in the distance. It calls to mind the light of a ship or a buoy on a dark sea.

"Is it him?" Emma asks, though of course there is no way to know.

"Let's find out," he says, and offers her his hand. She looks at it for a moment, then brings her gaze to meet his, both of their faces chalk-white in the moonlight. There is no apology in her eyes, but no anger either, only the acceptance, however temporary, of a truce for the greater good. Then she takes his hand, her skin cold, and they aim their flashlights ahead of them and plunge into the woods.

4

I N THE THICK OF THE TREES, the ground begins to rise again, which is not good. It tells Mike they are moving even further off track (wherever the hell the track *is*), ascending the moonshadow hill instead of descending to the valley where the chance of finding the campground is greater. But that's all right for now, because there is a light, the first one they've seen since losing their way. Best case scenario, it *is* Cody, demonstrating better sense than his parents did and waiting instead of roaming aimlessly through the enormous woods in search of them. If it's not, then Mike knows his heart is going to shatter and Emma will be inconsolable, but it might be a cabin, and from there they might be able to summon help and end this nightmare. And though he does not want to think about rescue choppers and search teams, and the horrifying possibility of never finding their son (especially considering what he and Emma will forever remember doing when they should have been looking for him), he wants even less to wander these woods indefinitely waiting to freeze or starve to death. His wife's words come back to him: *I still can't believe it's even possible to get lost in this day and age.* And while of course such a thing is possible—it happens all the time—he didn't think it possible *here*, not in a stretch of woods less than an hour from their home. Abroad, maybe, where everything would seem alien, but not here, not somewhere he could probably see the Columbus skyline if he climbed high enough.

But all he has seen for the past three hours, and all he fears he will ever see again, are more and more trees.

"You all right?" he asks his wife, and she looks at him, her face barely lit by the glow from her flashlight.

"No," she replies.

They're cold and miserable and out of their depth, the tension between them far from eradicated, only on hold for the time being. The argument both incensed and demoralized him, like ice water thrown on a burning man, leaving him numb, and now he finds himself investing everything he has left in that little light. It might be a lantern, his son's or a hunter's flashlight, a candle in the window of a welcoming home or a manned outpost...it is not yet possible to tell. But what it represents is a promise of sanctuary, however temporary, and so they skid and strain their way against the rocky, slippery slope, heartened by its unwavering glow.

It takes them the better part of forty minutes before the slope levels out and they find themselves in a clearing. There they stop, exhausted. Mike doubles over, hands on his knees, his heart hammering so hard it must surely be digging its way out of his chest, while Emma surveys the area.

"Cory?" she says, her voice low, as if afraid of disturbing someone.

Ringed by gnarled and ancient oak trees, the clearing is roughly forty, no more than fifty feet in diameter, the floor carpeted with the same woodland detritus they've been battling their way through all night: twisted scrub, broken branches, twigs, and dead leaves, though here and there are bare patches of earth and what appear to be a scattering of small dark boulders. It is an unremarkable place, otherwise disappointing to Mike but for the tent that squats upon one of those patches. Once he has caught his breath, he straightens, knees, back, and feet aching, but does not move. Emma stands a few feet away from him, staring at the tent and similarly immobile, and though she doesn't say a word, he knows what has given her pause, can see it just as clearly as she can.

The tent is unlike any he has ever seen before, and yet somehow it reminds him of his own. Perhaps it is the dark yellow hue, or the dome-like shape, but there the similarities to his ill-advised purchase end. The longer he looks at it, the better it makes him feel about his own dubious skill as an outdoorsman, because clearly whoever erected this tent didn't even know that the tent poles or rods or whatever the heck they're called, usually go on the inside. Then again, the rods themselves don't look like the traditional kind either. Dark brown, ropy and knuckled, and curving down from an arched and similarly knuckled spine-like ridge along the top of the tent, they appear to be made from flexible sticks or branches, so Mike wonders if perhaps, rather than looking at the work of an amateur, he's observing the work of a *true* frontiersman, someone who perhaps, in losing their own tent in the inclement weather, had the resourcefulness to fashion a crude one from the materials at hand. The roof and sides of the tent appear to have been fashioned using vellum, or similar material, thin enough to allow the small orb of light within to be seen from without. There are no pegs or guy lines, and odder still, no entrance that he can see, though it's possible they're looking at the back of it.

Emma turns to look at him. "Do you think he might be in there?"

He doesn't, because the soft amber light inside the tent is unobstructed and casts no shadows against its walls, but he takes a moment to weigh up the wisdom of sharing this opinion. He settles for a noncommittal "Not sure," and takes a few steps further into the clearing and looks around even though there is little to be seen. "But if nothing else, it could be a place to stop and regroup." As soon as he uses the word, he regrets it, because the terrible truth is that their *group* is one short, and he knows that they were counting on finding Cody behind that light, beckoning them toward him with his flashlight. More than once, Mike even imagined he saw the boy's fuzzy silhouette waiting for them in the darkness behind that glow. But now they're here, and Cody isn't, and the implications of that fact are enough to suck the life from him, to hammer ingots of despair and hopelessness into his brain.

Please God, let him be all right. Whatever the price I need to pay, I'll gladly pay it. Just please, please, let my boy be okay.

But he refuses to give up, at least not yet. He has to hold it together for Emma's sake, for Cody's sake. Whatever happens, they need to stay alert and vigilant, need to focus on reclaiming their son from the cold, dark woods. Because if anything has happened to their boy, it will alter for them both the definition of lost. There will, quite simply, be no more reason for them to go on. They may have their differences, may even have to go their separate ways and concede defeat when all of this is over, but the boy is an innocent and should not be made to pay for his unflagging faith in his guardians, in the people sworn to protect him. If such faith ends up costing the boy his life, then Mike and Emma will be guilty of the ultimate failure, and it will kill them, and the punishment will fit the crime.

He turns his head and looks at the tent. "It didn't just pop up out of the ground," he mumbles.

Emma draws closer to him, her fingers finding the crook of his arm in a tenderness borne of anxiety, not love, from the accurate assumption that he has become just as fragile as she has. "What?"

"The tent. It'd be one thing if we just stumbled upon somebody's old abandoned camping ground, but the tent's in pretty good shape from what I can see, and there's a light on, which means somebody used it, and recently. And people don't just walk off and leave their stuff behind, right?" *Unless they're people like us*, he thinks miserably, picturing the backpack he left by the boulder somewhere down there at the foot of the hill, and the tent they abandoned, though technically the tent abandoned *them*. "So there's a good chance whoever owns this thing will come back, and they can help us."

Encouraged, Emma nods. "Okay, that makes sense."

In the distance, thunder rumbles. A light rain starts to fall, pattering like insistent fingers on their slickers.

"Shit," Mike says, feeling his spirits fall in time with the silvery threads. "Looks like the dry spell is over."

"Should we wait inside it?" Emma asks, training her flashlight beam at the side of the tent and bleaching out the interior amber glow. "I mean, you don't think whoever owns it would mind, do you? Considering the circumstances? At least we'd be out of the rain."

For a moment, Mike doesn't answer, because he doesn't know what to say other than that he doesn't think that's a good idea at all. Considering all that's gone wrong this night, the strange little tent is a godsend. And yet, for no reason he can express in words, the more he looks at it, the more he realizes that he would rather continue to brave the storm than crawl inside it. It's a preposterous thing to feel, and he knows this, and yet the potency of his sudden, inexplicable aversion to the tent seems justification enough.

You're being ridiculous.

This he knows, but still...

"I'm not sure that's the best idea," he says.

"For Heaven's sake, why?"

"I don't know, just a feeling. We don't know who owns it, or how they might react to finding us inside. Could be a hunter's camp."

"So?"

"The kind of hunter who might mistake us for scavengers and shoot before asking questions."

"Like it or not, we *are* scavengers now, Mike. And if there's food in there, I don't mind telling you, I'm going to help myself. Coffee, the same."

He has to admit the idea of sustenance sounds tempting. They haven't eaten anything since stopping at a Wendy's on their way to the hills. When was that? Five, six, hours ago? His mouth waters, his body prematurely warming to the thought of hot coffee gushing down his throat, melting the ice inside him and chasing away some of the dread.

And yet it is that same dread that holds him in place as he studies the yellow object with the odd branch-like trim. He notices it doesn't move, seems resistant to the wind.

Which is perhaps what a good, expensive, reliable tent does, *Mike, not that you'd know anything about it. Yours was a discount item because you were more concerned with your bank balance than the safety of your family. It's a tent, for God's sake, nothing more, and all you're doing now is all you've ever done: making dubious choices and stalling when affirmative action would yield a more sensible result,* chides the voice of reason, a voice that might have made Mike's life a whole lot better if he had acknowledged its counsel even once over the years. But instinct will not allow him to heed it now.

"Let's just wait a while, okay? Out here."

He knows she's going to argue, and doesn't blame her. The woods are getting to him. The cold and the rain and the hunger and the desperation have combined to make a scrambled mess of his brains. The enormity of what has happened to them, of what his misguided need to bond with his family has caused to happen is debilitating. The thought of waiting here while Cody wanders the woods alone and frightened is enough to make him want to tear his own heart out, but he doesn't know what else to do. His wife, like his own inner voice, will argue that he's circumventing wisdom, as always, making the situation more difficult than it already is. And she'll be right, and he will have no comeback. Because the only thing he can think to say will only make him appear insane, and even more pathetic than his actions thus far have allowed: *I'm afraid of it, Emma. The tent. I can't explain why so please don't ask me. It just feels wrong, feels like someone drew us here on purpose. One light in the whole damn woods, in a part of the woods nobody's supposed to go, and it leads us here, to a tent with nobody in it. It just feels wrong.*

"Out here?" Emma says. "So we can get soaked all over again. What's the matter with you?"

To give him time to compose a reply good enough to placate her—assuming such a reply exists—he carefully makes his way to the nearest one of the small boulders. He needs to sit down, to take the weight off his feet, because it feels as if the backs of his hiking boots have eaten their way clean through to the bone. But as he nears the boulder, he sees that it is not a boulder at all, but some kind of shrub. Closer still and his light reveals that it is more like tumbleweed, though more densely constructed and much bigger than any he has ever seen. It reaches almost to his waist.

"Emma, come take a look at this," he says, raising his light to shoulder height and aiming the beam downward like a mechanic inspecting the guts of a troublesome vehicle.

"What now?"

Despite the cold sensation of dread that crawls like the rain down the back of his neck, Mike is fascinated at his discovery.

The object before him is a rough oval composite of grass, sticks, and coarse thin fibers he identifies as animal hair, and as he runs a tentative hand over the top of the tightly woven mass, the twigs like hard, slick tendrils in the rain, he is once again transported via memory back to his youth, this time to Mrs. Edgerton's biology class on the day when she got them all to study owl pellets. He recalls being repulsed as he pulled apart the small, hairy brown orb of compacted waste matter, only to find his sense of wonder inflamed at the sight of what was revealed to him: several smooth tiny stones, desiccated insect remains, and the skeleton of a mouse. *Indigestible material,* Mrs. Edgerton had informed the class with her trademark haughty, holier-than-thou delivery, *which in its excretion also helps cleanse the gullet of the animal.*

Mike shakes his head. What he is looking at couldn't possibly be the same manner of thing, could it? *Not unless they have birds the size of my Toyota up here.* Deferring to that sense of childhood wonder again, he pins the flashlight under his chin, the light angled toward the top of the tumbleweed-thing, and braces his knees against the object for support—thereby discovering that it is heavy enough to resist being moved by his weight—and, carefully slipping his fingers into the latticework of branches of which the outer shell is composed, pulls the thing apart. It opens easily, the top portion splitting wide with the sound of firecrackers, and Mike stumbles back a step as a noxious smell of methane rises in an invisible cloud to envelop him. Coughing, he waves a hand before his face, eyes wide with incredulity, and, the flashlight trembling in his hand from the cocktail of cold, fatigue, and terror, leans over to inspect his handiwork.

"Honey..." he says, his voice very small. "You're not going to believe this..."

His efforts have not sundered the object enough for him to see straight down into its center. He has only managed to yank open an upper section of its bulk, but it's enough. On the tightly woven bed of straw, wiry animal hair, and undigested plant matter he has exposed, the light shows a large portion of bone, and perhaps it is only because he has already summoned the memory of his high school biology class that he understands that the bone, scratched and striated and shiny in the rain, does not belong to an animal.

But the red collar with the little silver bell most certainly does.

He straightens, moves away from the giant pellet-thing and slowly sweeps his juddering flashlight beam to his left, to the three other "boulders" he registered on the way in, then to his right, where there are two more, laying on their sides like giant, dark

Easter eggs. From one of them pokes what he earlier took to be the dead branch of a silver birch and now acknowledges is more likely the leg-bone of an animal, probably a deer. A cold current floods through his body. And in his shock, the only thing that runs through his mind is a simple, logical fact, a ridiculously obvious observation that nonetheless terrifies him to his core.

Waste follows feeding.

He takes another step backward, his throat clenching against the magnificently irresistible need to scream until his lungs burst, because now he knows something else. Cavemen did not need prior knowledge or textbooks or common sense to know when they were being hunted. They felt it on an instinctual, primal level. And that, he concludes, even as his composure threatens to collapse like a shoddily built wall, is what *he* felt as soon as they stepped foot into the clearing.

"Hello?" he hears his wife ask, and knows it is not directed at him. The sound of that word paints a picture of what he's going to see when he turns around and his body goes rigid. Because even though what he has just found is not sufficient evidence to identify the tent as the source of the danger he feels crawling all over him now like an army of fire ants, instinct tells him it is, and it is on this instinct he realizes he should have relied.

"Emma," he says. "Don't."

"I found the opening," she replies.

His paralysis breaks and he turns, his flashlight sweeping an arc of luminescence through the rain. "Emma, no!"

She is down on her haunches, pulling back a large leathery flap at the far end of the tent, the end that was hidden from them when they entered the clearing. The look on her face as she does so does nothing to assuage his dread. It is a look of repulsion, one he has come to know very well for all the wrong reasons during the course of his marriage to this woman, and when she releases the flap, it remains connected to her fingers by long thick translucent strands of mucous. And although he feels himself running to her, reaching out to grab her and yank her away from there, he can't move. In what is perhaps a sign of impending insanity, the voice inside his head becomes that of the marriage counselor, that enviably handsome Doctor White, with the perfect teeth and expensive clothes, who probably never had problems with a woman, or a man, for that matter, in his whole damn life, saying words he never would have said out loud:

You've wanted to run for years, haven't you Mike. You've just never had the courage.

No, that isn't—

And now you can. Because this situation doesn't require courage. Just the opposite. All you need to do here is give in to your instinctual need for self-preservation, and run. Problem solved.

No. I won't. I can't.

Sure you can. Because as much an outsider as you may have always felt, you're out of your element for real right here. This isn't your world. People are forbidden from coming here for a very good reason. And right now, you're looking at it. This, Mikey, is most definitely Not Your Department.

Mike drops the flashlight and, screaming his wife's name, runs toward the tent, his heels and shins raging with pain, the panic in his throat threatening to strangle him. And as he closes the distance, he sees Emma, the woman he knows he loves despite her doubts, the counselor's doubts, and even his own, look up at him in confusion, her hands still held out before her in disgust, the glistening mess dripping from between her fingers. In an instant, at the sight of him, his primal terror is transferred to her eyes. Swallowing, unwilling to wait to find out why her husband is hobbling toward her in insane panic, she starts to stand.

"Mike, what—?"

The back end of the tent deflates as if crushed under the foot of an invisible giant. At the same time, the ridged spine, so like a thorny branch, arches itself and the flaps at the front snap open like batwings, partially obscuring what happens next.

Emma screams; Mike stumbles over a knotted mess of branches and goes down, badly scraping his hands and knees, and the tent begins to shudder.

Up on his tortured feet again and he's alongside the thing, almost within grabbing distance of his wife, close enough now to see that the soft light inside the tent-that-is-not-a-tent is glowing like a sun, close enough to see the network of thin, dark blue veins threading like worms through its vellum-like skin, close enough to hear his wife draw in a breath to scream.

But the scream never comes. Like a javelin thrown with great force from inside the tent, a long wormy, segmented appendage with an end that tapers to a wickedly sharp point of bone explodes from inside the thing and punctures his wife's throat just below her larynx. She jolts, her eyes opening wide as moons that stare upward at nothing. She convulses, feet kicking at the ground and releases the breath in a gurgle that forces red bubbles out around the spike of bone that has penetrated her. The appendage shudders as if in desire as Emma's body sags, the life draining away even as her mucous-slimed hands beat weakly at the thing that has invaded her, but her protests are feeble and short-lived.

For a moment, it seems to Mike as if the world has been paused. Even the rain seems to slow. He drops to his knees, knowing he could still reach out and grab Emma's hand, knowing too that it's too late. In a panic, he sleeves tears away from his eyes, fearing they will blind him to some supernatural reversal of this horrific moment, or to some opportunity to undo it, and sees only the retraction of that appendage, withdrawn as quickly as it came, pulling his wife off her knees as if she were a rag doll. And then she is gone, with a small pool of blood the only sign that she was there at all, and the rain works hard to erase even that. The tent begins to undulate, the light within flickering and throwing the shadow of his wife against its skin as it feeds on her. His wife, and a hint of what murdered her.

At the sight of it, he feels or imagines he feels a small pop as the bubble of his sanity breaks, and an involuntary sob escapes him.

As if in response, the undulation of the tent halts.

Listening.

Mike claps his hands over his mouth, one over the other, madness and stark, raving terror pulsing between his eyes.

He cannot move, cannot breathe, doesn't dare. All he can do is watch, as, after a prolonged moment, the creature resumes its feeding. And as the rain grows heavier, each drop that taps against his head brings with it words he has learned in the years since Mrs. Edgerton's biology class. Words like: *bioluminescence, lure, camouflage, adaptation, imitation,* and perhaps just as accurate: *stingray, scorpion, crawfish, bat, arachnid.* None of these attributes or comparisons seems outlandish to him now, for in the shadow theater the interior of the tent-that-is-not-a-tent has become, he sees the impression of something that is all of these things and none of them. The large black mass at the epicenter calls to mind a fat black spider in its web, legs working busily as it rends his wife's body asunder, the bulk of its body extending down from the ridged spine. Spindly, knuckled arms connect bat-like to the sides (wings?) of the tent. Looking at it in its real form, Mike wonders how anyone could have mistaken it for something benign, but then, isn't that the point of camouflage? How many others, he wonders, as he slowly, ever-so-slowly rises to his feet, have gotten lost in the storm and been lured to their deaths at this creature's hands/claws/wings by the promise of shelter?

The answer, he supposes, lie in the tumbleweed-like mounds around him.

And it is to one of these mounds that he moves, limping around the puddles, careful to make as little noise as possible.

Facing the tent-thing, but averting his eyes as his wife's blood splashes the inside of its membranous walls and the thing shudders in ecstasy, he tries to keep the shock from turning him to stone.

It's okay to run now, Mr. Sellers, says the counselor.

"No, it isn't," Mike whispers. "It never was. And the first thing I'm going to do when, and if, I get back to Columbus, is punch your perfect fucking teeth in."

The counselor is quiet, and Mike finds solace in his anger, finds that it is all he has left. As he inches away from the tent toward the mound nearest the point where he and Emma entered the clearing, he tries not to think of Cody, because whenever he does, he sees him not as he was in life, but as a collection of stained and scratched undigested bones nestled in a clotted ovum of this creature's waste. As likely a fate as that might be, Mike refuses to believe it until confirmation presents itself, assuming it ever does. If there is a modicum of relief to be found in the chaotic nightmare his world has become, it is that the bone he saw inside that mound was adult-sized.

Cody then, might yet be alive, and this alone is reason enough to even consider resistance in the face of such an impossible aberration.

When he bumps up against one of the mounds, he stops, and reluctantly casts a glance at the tent. Blinks his eyes clear of the worsening rain. Whatever is left of his wife is not anything resembling a human now. The silhouette of the spider/crawfish/bat-thing is poking with spindly legs at a ragged, shapeless shadow it holds in its clutches, as if testing its tenderness.

Mike, trembling uncontrollably, and wishing the calm he felt were a good thing instead of an obvious sign that he has jumped headlong into the abyss he has feared as long as he's been on the earth, drops his gaze to the sodden ground between his feet, and the long leg-bone he spotted earlier. This close, it looks smaller and thinner, but given the circumstances, he figures it will be better than harsh words as a weapon. He drops down and tugs the bone free from the tangled latticework of the creature's waste, wonders as he rises if he has time to try and break it, to make it sharper, wonders if there's any point. And then he realizes it is not a bone at all, but a lovingly carved walking stick with a knuckled top. Remembers his own grandfather having a similar one, though perhaps it was a little less intricate and well-cared for as this one. Remembers because the old man used to hit him across the back with it when he was drunk. *You're just as worthless as your father, you little shit.* And the memory angers him.

And what do you plan to do with that? the counselor pipes up, sounding sulky from his earlier chastisement. *What do you think it will let you do with it? It'll snatch it away from you and use it to pick pieces of you and your poor wife from between its teeth.*

"Sh-shut up," Mike says, through chattering teeth.

Why not just throw stones at it instead?

Mike begins to limp his way back toward the tent, his body numb but his senses honed to the same sharp point absent from his weapon, as they must be when facing death. Emma is dead, Cody is missing, and no matter what hope he might try to siphon from the situation, on the only level resistant to denial, he knows everything is lost. His world, which he has fooled himself into thinking has always been some broad, endless thing, has been reduced to this clearing, and the thing that lives here, the hostile creature that has removed from him all that ever mattered. And though he is aware that the chances of inflicting damage on the creature are practically nonexistent—he imagines that appendage shooting out and killing him before he even has a chance to draw back the walking stick—there is quite simply nothing left to do. If he runs, if he was able enough to run, it would be on him in an instant. And even if it turns out that the malevolent thing is confined to this clearing and as such cannot give chase—so what? What kind of life awaits him now outside of this killing ground, beyond the place where everything was taken from him in a few short hours? No, he led his family into this horror, into this slaughter, and without them, there is no reason to leave.

Because instinct tells him his son is dead. He has not explored the other mounds, nor will he. The odds of his son's survival, already significantly reduced when they lost him, are, in the face of the unexpected horror these woods have been hiding, now practically nonexistent.

So here it must end, with a being he would never have dared believe existed outside of mad fantasy, a creature that if he were forced to describe to any rational person would no doubt elicit laughter and doubts about his sanity. They would label him a murderer because it would be the logical verdict. *No, Officer, it wasn't me, it was a tent!* He snorts involuntary laughter and then raises his free hand to stifle it. But it's difficult because indeed his enemy, the true murderer, *is* a laughable, incredible thing. But quickly the humor ebbs away, replaced by that welcome numbness as he brings his gaze to bear on the monster before him.

In the flesh, what he's looking at is not funny in the least. It is the stuff of nightmare, of the horror shows his mother kept on mute. And how he wishes he could mute all of this now, just shut out the world and wait for the broadcast to end and his life to go off the air.

Not for your ears, Mikey.

And not for his eyes.

Five feet from the tent, the light inside it goes out, and the creature is still.

Mike stops too, his breath coming in harsh rasps that send clouds of vapor steaming into the air, heating his cheeks only briefly. The rain continues to sizzle down around him. Uncertainty keeps him immobile, and faced with the abruptly dormant antagonist, a feeble red pulse of panic flares deep within him.

I could run. He envisions himself dropping the walking stick—and he admits now that he is in complete if reluctant agreement with the counselor regarding its efficacy as a weapon—and quietly making his way out of the clearing, imagines the darkness between the trees appearing to go on forever, walking for miles in the rain, defeated, drained by grief. And then a light, a break in the trees, another clearing, only this time the light that finds him is not the insidious lure of some unknowable predator, but the real light of a log cabin, its chimney trailing smoke he can smell from where he stands, dumbfounded. He sees the cabin door opening, revealing the firelight within, and a man standing in the doorway, beckoning him inside. And behind that man, perhaps being tended to by his kindly wife, a boy sits swaddled in a blanket sipping from a mug of hot chocolate. Cody. His son. Alive.

The tent moves.

Startled, Mike takes a panicked step backward.

Go, if you're going, he tells himself. *The window is closing.*

Body juddering from the force of his own heartbeat, Mike's grip on the walking stick tightens. He looks down to his right, to his flashlight lying forgotten on the ground, the beam directed forward at the tent. He rehearses the steps it will take to grab it and hobble his way out of there through the dark between the trees on the opposite side of the clearing. But then that instinct, so prevalent since first they stumbled upon the clearing, returns, and this time it has a very simple message for him, one he can read as clear as a neon sign through the rain: *Too late.*

Whatever opportunity there might have been up until now, it has passed.

The flashlight is too far away to risk retrieving it. Instead, he unzips one of the pockets in his slicker and plucks out his phone. His hand is trembling so violently, it takes him three tries to hit the

ON button. Two seconds later, it glows to life with a hum of vibration and a cheery series of tones that have no place in a situation so grim. A clumsy but hasty series of swipes and button-presses on the rain-smeared screen and he chooses his FLASHLIGHT app, previously only used to help him find dropped items in the car at night, now a potentially life-saving tool in circumstances he doubts the manufacturers ever predicted. The strength of the light as it flares from the back of the phone puts the abandoned flashlight to shame. As he sweeps the blazing blue beam up and out toward the tent, it unveils itself before him, as if it, perhaps possessed by some perverse love for the theatrical, has been waiting for the spotlight to do that very thing.

Mike forgets to breathe as the whole tent flattens and the front folds back like a hood, exposing a pale white triangular shape that might be an angular head with blind, boiled egg eyes. Long thin jaws with curved and curiously blunt yellow teeth snap at the clouds of breath that spume from its narrow throat, and Mike gets another whiff of methane, or perhaps sulfur. The vellum walls of the tent rise up and out before collapsing to the saturated ground with a splash as if abandoning the idea of flight, like kites in a day that has lost its breath. The wings, heavily veined and shaped like those he has seen in illustrations of dragons, now lie flat at right angles to its body, and he can see small thorny nicotine-colored protrusions along the ridge of the wing closest to him. In the center of the creature's mass, beneath its knuckled spine, the skin ripples as something moves beneath it, the same arachnid-like thing he glimpsed in silhouette, the thing that killed his wife. The bulbous light, the lure, pulsates as if in warning, or alarm. For a moment, the cow skull-like head of the creature seems to writhe in protest or in pain, its wings beating clumsily and uselessly at the ground, spattering Mike with rain water. And though he can't be certain of anything given his pedestrian knowledge of such matters, a suspicion floats up through the murk of horror in Mike's mind: He is not looking at one creature, but two, one of them feeding off the other, controlling it. A parasite and its host.

Before he can discover what that parasite might be advising its host to do next, Mike braces himself and allows all the terror, the grief, and the rage to come rushing up from the core of him. The resulting maelstrom of adrenaline is as unknown to him as a foreign language being whispered into his ear, as alien as his enemy, and with a lunatic scream, he closes the distance between them with a series of ungainly steps, and throws himself on top of the flailing creature. He is immediately struck by the fetid stench of the thing and the repulsive feel of its skin against his own. It is like nylon coated in glue and as he scrambles for purchase, tries to dig his nails into its skin, it thrashes beneath him. Struggling not to slide or be thrown free of the creature, thereby losing the only advantage he might get, he brings the walking stick up high, his gaze fixated on the agitated movement in the center of the creature's mass, the engine fueling this horror, the spider-thing that tore his wife from him, and, teeth clenched, brings the stick down with every ounce of strength he has left. It connects with a satisfying crunch, and the skin above it rips, allowing the light to shine through. It is pulsating faster now, and darkening to an orangey-red. The parasite does not make a sound, but wrenches itself away, which has the simultaneous effect of forcing the larger creature to do the same. And when it does, the wing to which Mike clings pulls away, revealing the ground underneath, and any sense of victory he might have felt is quashed as his grip begins to slacken and he begins to slide. Because there *is* no ground underneath, only a deep dark hole, the hole he suspects with mounting horror is the place from which this creature—both of them—came, their ecology forced aboveground perhaps by their own conflict, or hunger, or by man. Such questions will never be answered for Mike, or anyone else, unless these monstrosities grow bolder still and force themselves out further into the world.

He tries to push himself free of the creature, tries to get his feet beneath him, but this, he suspects, is part of the creature's design, a backup plan in case of attack. It has been here for however long, squatting over the hole, safeguarding it, staying close to the only form of egress that makes any sense, while luring in idiot humans.

And how like an idiot Mike feels now as he continues to slide, the foul stench of it filling his nose.

When did it first come, he wonders? *When did it crawl from its subterranean lair, and what did it see when it did? Was it frightened, determined, hungry?* He imagines it waiting in the dark, studying the only other source of light in the dark woods—a yellow tent with a light burning within. Perhaps despite being a creature of the Stygian dark, light is a language it understands. And so, it adopts the pose of a tent and sends out its signal in the hope of communicating with this other strange creature. But its only response was to send along the creatures that were hiding inside it. And perhaps once it devoured them, it mulled over the gesture and considered it a gift, for indeed it had been starving.

The creature flails; Mike slips further, hands scrabbling madly for purchase where there is none to be found. The orangey-red light burns crimson. He has wounded the parasite, he's sure of it, but his only reward for his boldness, will be death.

He has time only to pray for a mankind who never knew him that the day will never come in which such creatures grow bold enough to leave this place, and then he is clawing at the wing, thrusting his feet out toward the edges of the ragged hole in one last attempt to save himself, his efforts undone as the creature rises up on its side at the behest of the parasite.

But I did it, Mike thinks, with one single moment of shining pride. *I attacked it, wounded it, maybe killed it. I didn't run. For once, I didn't run.*

There is a brief tantalizing moment in which his fall is halted, the heel of one foot pinned by his own weight and impetus against the grassy edge of the dark hole, his back braced reflexively against the creature's bulk. His mind goes blank. No thoughts, only a flat-line of primal dread laced with acceptance, and a cold electric current that hums through him from groin to sternum, until the parasite bids its host to move again, his foot slips, and the world opens like a hungry mouth beneath him and he is falling.

5

THE FALL SEEMS TO LAST FOR AN ETERNITY, the abyss endless and impenetrably dark. As the air whistles past his ears, he hears first the walking stick, then his phone, splash against the bottom, and is absurdly relieved to know there is one. That there's water suggests he might survive the fall. The odds are not good that he won't simply shatter himself against the rocks, but any odds are better than none.

He is no longer afraid, no longer anything but an empty vessel with one word left on his lips: *Sorry.*

The word is meant for Emma, for Cody, for himself, until he has the opportunity to tell them face to face in whatever follows oblivion, assuming anything does.

The promise of it gives him a smile.

Sixty feet down, a tall thin stalagmite abruptly halts his descent, punching through his stomach, shattering his lower vertebrae, and suspending him there in the dark like a fly on a needle. The pain feels like something bestowed upon someone else. He is already dying, finally ready to exit a world that was Not His Department.

Soon, his beloved mother comes and mercifully mutes the world for her little boy, one last time.

6

O N THE OPPOSITE SIDE OF THE CLEARING, unexplored by Mike or his ill-fated wife, the hill slopes downward through another two miles of dense, tangled woodland. A disused and therefore untrustworthy slatted wooden rope-bridge crosses a narrow river which, if followed south for another quarter-mile, leads to the approved camping ground Mike eschewed despite the camp attendant's instructions.

As the sun rises on the new day like a swollen, burning pumpkin, turning to sparkling diamonds the beads of water left in the wake of the storm and coaxing veils of mist up from the sodden earth, Greg Kohl, a fifty-three-year-old college lecturer, emerges from his tent and stretches. Refreshed despite a sleep frequently interrupted by volleys of thunder and the howling wind, he sets about making coffee for himself and his girlfriend, Karen, a girl who is thirty years his junior, a revelation in the sack, and the third girl he has brought up here in the past ten months. With no one to answer to up here but his own ego, he permits himself a satisfied grin, and, as he sets up the camp stove, replays the memory of Karen's nubile body, and the various creative ways in which she let him use it.

When he realizes there is a kid standing less than two feet away from him, he starts, almost burns himself on the camp stove and curses, then, as he takes in the face of his visitor, immediately wishes he hadn't.

The kid looks like something from a documentary about the Serbian war. His clothes are caked in mud and soaking wet, as if he spent the night in the woods, in the rain. He is shivering violently, his teeth making audible clicking sounds. In the oval of his dirty face, his eyes are wide, the pupils amid the blue shrunken down to pinpoints. The kid has his arms down by his sides, the index fingers of both hands tapping against his palms, as if he thinks he's playing a videogame.

"Hey," Greg says, and rises. "You okay, kid?"

It's a ridiculous question, because clearly the kid isn't, but he's not sure what else to say. Greg swallows, tries to think, something that's never easy for him in the pre-coffee stages of his mornings, and especially with the hangover that's pounding against the walls of his skull like a lunatic inmate. But something is wrong here. The kid before him looks the very definition of haunted, so he knows he has to do something, become the conscientious, helpful adult, even though he'd rather just crawl back inside the tent and curl up beside the lovely Karen Wilkes.

"What's your name?" he asks, because that seems as good a place to start as any.

The kid just stands there, lips dry and cracked and sealed like a scar, watching him.

"Did something happen?" Another dumb question, but Greg is at a loss. So he raises a finger, as if he has lost his voice too, or as if he thinks the child might respond better to non-verbalized communication, indicating that the kid should wait, and he ducks back inside the tent. It reeks of sex, stale perfume, and alcohol. Karen, little more than a tangle of blonde hair on her inflatable pillow, moans and rolls over, squints up at him, her mascara smudged around her eyes, making her look significantly less attractive than he found her last night. Her sleeping bag is wrapped tightly around her, but there's no missing the half-moons of her large, surgically enhanced breasts over the material. It's the first time he's been with someone who has fake breasts, and he does not consider himself a fan. Wild horses could not drag that admission out of him, however, for Greg is a man who is thankful for the women his charm and money and position of authority affords him, particularly considering his ugly, and ongoing, marital dissolution.

"What's going on?" she mumbles, throwing a hand with French-manicured fingernails over her eyes.

"I need a blanket," Greg tells her. "Some kid's in trouble."

"Trouble?"

"Yeah. Go back to sleep. I'll take care of it."

"And then me?" She smiles sleepily, another hint of the neediness she has been displaying on and off since they violated the teacher-student rule and became an item.

"Yeah, and you," he promises, and yanks the spare blanket off her.

"Boo. So cold," she says, and rolls over.

Ever the humanitarian, Greg thinks, and exits the tent.

The kid is right where he left him, still standing there shivering and looking shell-shocked. Greg can't help wondering about the nature of his ordeal. Was he in a car crash? Get lost in the woods? See something terrible? Or is he just some local yokel's kid, wandered down out of the mountains to bug the regular folk for money or food. The theme song to *Deliverance* twangs through his head and he has to struggle to suppress a smile.

"Here kid," he says and holds the blanket up to indicate his intent.

The kid backs away. Greg stops, frowns.

"You're freezing. Let me put the blanket on you and we'll get you some coffee and figure out what to do next, okay?"

The kid gives no sign that he understands, which leads Greg to the conclusion that whatever the boy has been through, it was bad. He decides the best course of action after getting the kid warm, is to get to the camping office down the trail and either wait for the attendant to show, or see if there's an emergency number he can call. Someone must be looking for the kid, after all.

Again, he tries to swoop the blanket like a cape around the kid's shoulders, and almost manages it this time, one half of it coming down on the backpack that's slung over the boy's shoulders. But as soon as the material hits the pack, the kid winces and backs away. It is the first sign of emotion the child has shown, and it alarms Greg, who takes it as an indication that the boy is wounded. After a moment of indecision, he lets the blanket fall to the ground.

"Okay," he says. "Will you let me take a look? If you're hurt, I might be able to help."

How he might be able to help when his area of expertise is American History is anybody's guess, but he needs to get the kid to trust him, to let him at least gauge the extent of the trouble he, and by association, Greg, is in.

"Easy now." As he starts to move slowly and carefully toward the boy, hands raised to show he means no harm, he finds himself surprised at the situation in which he has found himself, for while he's reluctant to call himself a selfish man, the last few years of his life have seen him dedicating the lion's share of his efforts to pursuits designed solely to benefit nobody but himself. Call it the fallout from a life spent trying to be fair and equal, with little reward. That he didn't immediately try to slough the responsibility for this kid off on someone, *any*one else, or just go back into the tent and zip it up when he first encountered him, is certainly not in keeping with his character. *My good deed for the day*, he decides.

A quick look around at the campsite reveals that all but one of the other couples have already packed up and left, and the only sign of life from the remaining tent is a soft, droning snore. Greg wonders if he should rouse the other couple. He recalls the wife being pretty hot too, even if she was closer to his age and showing every last bit of it. The husband was a quiet type, so maybe the wife might be impressed by Greg's heroics and therefore amenable to a little three-way extra-marital fun with Synthetic Karen, assuming they could find a way to get rid of hubby for a while.

Jesus, he tells himself. *What's the matter with you?*

With a grin, he shakes his head. *The age-old question, hombre, but what fun it is pursuing the answer.*

The kid is close enough for him to touch now, and stiffens, raises his shoulders. Head bowed, he looks up at Greg from beneath a furrowed brow and the ragged theater wings of his damp hair.

"I'm not going to hurt you," Greg tells him. "I promise. But if you're hurt, I want to help you, understand?"

Again, no indication from the boy that he understands anything, but despite his defensive posture, he does not move away this time, and Greg takes that as a positive sign. He slowly moves around the boy, inspecting his neck for bruises or wounds, and sees nothing but fish-belly white skin, the shivering intensifying.

"There's nothing to be afraid of," Greg says in the same comforting, disarming tone he uses to such great effect on his dates. The backpack is covered in a thick layer of slowly drying mud, the weight of which goes some way toward explaining the discomfort on the child's face when the blanket touched it. God knows how far the poor kid trekked with all that crap on his back.

"First things first," he says, "Let's get this thing off you."

The kid goes rigid, turns to stone, but Greg figures it's now or never and quickly grabs the sides of the backpack, intending to lift it up to relieve the boy of his burden.

A moment of confusion as the backpack, much heavier than he anticipated, moves liquidly beneath Greg's fingers, as if he has grabbed a slimy bag of fish, and he grimaces as the mud begins to slough off around and through his fingers. Repulsed as he is, he decides it is better to keep going. Dropping something this heavy back down on the kid's back might send him sprawling. That would be the perfect time for the other couple to poke their heads out of the tent, wouldn't it? *Hey*, he imagines them yelling at him, *leave that poor kid alone.*

"Jesus," he hisses through his teeth. "What have you got in here, kid, rocks?"

An inch from the boy's flesh, and the backpack snags on something, something that resists Greg's efforts, and no matter how hard he pulls, it refuses to yield to him.

The boy lowers his head further, begins to sob, and Greg feels a rush of guilt.

I'm hurting him. I should just—

It is at that moment that he catches of glimpse of what's holding the pack in place. It's something black and knuckled, like a long, thin, spindly twig, and it appears to be buried in the boy's shoulder.

More of the mud slides off, splattering Greg's shoes. He doesn't notice.

"What the fuck?" he asks, forgetting himself, as he hoists up the other side of the backpack as far as it will go, as much as it will let him, and notes another of the black knuckled sticks on that side too, the length of it seeming to sprout from the pack into a raw red puncture wound on the boy's back, connecting one to the other.

The backpack moves, and with a cry of fright, Greg releases it, and watches the boy stagger forward a step before its weight.

"I don't know..." Greg says, appalled. "I just...what the hell is that thing, kid?"

His mind floods with images of child torturers and abusive parents, of weird cults, and maniacs, and still he shakes his head. He has been alive for half a century and has never encountered anything like this.

And then he notices something hanging from the underside of the backpack, at the small of the boy's back. At first glimpse it appears to be a water vessel of some kind, but it looks too fleshy for that, and although he has no problem admitting that there is a lot he doesn't know about the world, one thing he's pretty sure of is that canteens don't glow, or look like plant bulbs. And as he watches, his hand straying to his brow as if to contain his confusion, the light begins to pulsate.

First: amber.

The child's shuddering worsens.

Then orange.

The boy falls to his knees as the backpack, presented with a more formidable, mature, and therefore infinitely more useful host, begins to detach itself with the sound of a Velcro strap being torn away.

Then red.

And Greg Kohl, who has spent his last few years looking out only for himself, abruptly finds himself in service to another.

7

FORTY-FIVE MINUTES LATER, Danielle Miller, the camp attendant, arrives at work with a hangover that would have rivaled Greg Kohl's in potency. And like the recently *appropriated* Mr. Kohl, Danielle's thoughts are fixated this day on her partner, namely the girl she will, this coming weekend, be bringing to meet her folks for the first time. She suspects her mother will be shocked, but understanding, when she learns of her precious daughter's sexual preference. She suspects her father will disown her. But the time for hiding, for lying and pretending she's something she is not, and never has been, is over. And if the cost of liberation and honesty is the love of her father, then so be it. It will just mean that all those years of him claiming he would love her no matter what she did in life will make him the liar.

She pulls into the parking lot and kills the engine, sits for a moment in the stillness which is always her favorite part of the day. This is her second year working here, and so perhaps she no longer appreciates the beauty of the area as much as she once did, as others do, but she will always appreciate the quiet. Particularly today when she knows her bold claims about her father are not entirely true. She loves him, and always will. And she knows he loves her too. She just wants more than anything for him to surprise her, to support her, to let them all move on as if nothing's changed, because for Danielle, they haven't.

She steps out of the car and grabs the brown bag containing the lunch Erica packed for her. The contents thrill her not at all. She'd much rather a double cheeseburger and fries from the nearby Wendy's than the turkey wrap and kale chips, but they have a dieting pact and she's determined not to be the first one to cave. She'll still be starving afterward, but isn't that the point of a diet?

With a slight smile at the image of her beautiful Erica chastising her for her thoughts of insubordination, she slams the car door, noting the presence of the old Toyota among the few vehicles remaining in the lot, and lets herself into the office. As it always has since it was first built, it smells of freshly cut timber, a smell she adores. Tossing her unappealing lunch on the chipped and scarred table, she goes to the window that grants a view of the trail and the camping ground at the crest of the hill.

She prays today of all days that she won't have to listen to the campers bitching about last night's storm, as if she could have done anything to prevent it.

Then her heart sinks as a gust of wind across the campsite sends fallen material waving to her like a red hand.

Shit. Of the two tents remaining in camp, one has fallen, victim, she assumes, of the storm. With a sigh of irritation, she realizes her hope that the owners left in the night as soon as the going got rough was a naïve one. She did warn them of the impending storm, after all. Told them it might be better to come back tomorrow. But those owners, a perv professor and his girlfriend—who looked young enough to be his daughter—clearly had other things on their minds to be bothered by such trivial things as caution.

She's about to move away from the window when, as if summoned by her thoughts of him, down the trail comes the creepy professor, the one who looked at her like a starving man looks at a rotisserie chicken when he checked in, his bespectacled eyes addressing her breasts as if they were doing the talking. He is disheveled and wearing what looks like a large muddy backpack, the weight of it clearly affecting his balance.

"Great," she groans, encouraged even less by the stilted walk and pallid face of the man as he clomps his way toward the office, his expression like a man who has just received the worst kind of news. *Probably still drunk.*

What she cannot yet see from her limited viewpoint are the small, faintly glowing, egg-like sores that are already beginning to surface around the professor's throat. When she does register them, she will assume they are burns sustained from some kind of accident. She will only realize her mistake when those boils pop and send their contents into her eyes and open mouth.

And Danielle will forget her diet in favor of a whole different kind of sustenance.

"So much for a hassle-free day," she murmurs to herself, as she scoops up her keys and goes out to meet the professor.

8

I N THE POOL AT THE BOTTOM OF THE SHAFT dug by the
creature at the behest of its puppeteer, its winged, flightless,
dragon-like brethren swim in crude circles, blind and oblivious
to the presence of the dead man impaled upon the stalagmite above
them, but excited by the blood that rains down from Up There, a
place the parasites attached to their undersides tell them they will
one day visit for themselves...

...while Up There, Greg the professor and Danielle, no longer
driven by compulsions of their own, sit into their respective
vehicles and shut the doors. They wait. Soon after, they are joined
by the Professor's girlfriend, and the couple from the other tent:
Stan and Marcy Hopkins, all of them called to the parking lot by the
parasite, all of them wearing faintly glowing necklaces of the
creature's incubating spawn. For a while none of them do anything
but sit stock-still and listen to their new and merciless internal
voices. Occasionally pain flickers across their faces as the parasite
punishes their attempts to resist its influence, secreting painful
toxins into their bloodstream until once more they are forced to
obey, and rewarding them with brief surges of endorphins when
they do.

At length, and in perfect synchronicity, bidden by commands
clearer to them than the voices of their own muted consciences, the
egg sacs pulsing brighter as the creature nourishes its young in

preparation for the hatching, Danielle, Greg, and Stan start up their vehicles and slowly reverse out of the campground parking lot.

Beyond the narrow lanes and the twisting mountain roads, the city awaits, unaware of the alien threat that will soon infect its veins.

The parasite shivers in anticipation as they clear the shadow of the mountain it has called home for a hundred thousand years.

ABOUT THE AUTHOR

Born and raised in a small harbor town in the south of Ireland, Kealan Patrick Burke knew from a very early age that he was going to be a horror writer. The combination of an ancient locale, a horror-loving mother, and a family full of storytellers, made it inevitable that he would end up telling stories for a living. Since those formative years, he has written five novels, over a hundred short stories, six collections, and edited four acclaimed anthologies. In 2004, he was honored with the Bram Stoker Award for his novella *The Turtle Boy.*

Kealan has worked as a waiter, a drama teacher, a mapmaker, a security guard, an assembly-line worker at Apple Computers, a salesman (for a day), a bartender, landscape gardener, vocalist in a grunge band, curriculum content editor, fiction editor at *Gothic.net,* associate editor at *Subterranean* magazine, and, most recently, a fraud investigator.

When not writing, Kealan designs book covers through his company Elderlemon Design.

A number of his books have been optioned for film.

Visit him on the web at www.kealanpatrickburke.com

NOW AVAILABLE in DIGITAL and PAPERBACK

BLANKY

In the wake of his infant daughter's tragic death, Steve Brannigan is struggling to keep himself together. Estranged from his wife, who refuses to be inside the house where the unthinkable happened, and unable to work, he seeks solace in an endless parade of old sitcoms and a bottle of bourbon.

Until one night he hears a sound from his daughter's old room, a room now stripped bare of anything that identified it as hers...except for her security blanket, affectionately known as Blanky.

Blanky, old and frayed, with its antiquated patchwork of badly sewn rabbits with black button eyes, who appear to be staring at the viewer...

Blanky, purchased from a strange old man at an antique stall selling "BABY CLOSE" at a discount.

The presence of Blanky in his dead daughter's room heralds nothing short of an unspeakable nightmare that threatens to take away what little light remains in Steve's shattered world

Because his daughter loved Blanky so much, he buried her with it.

A new novella from the Bram Stoker Award-Winning author of SOUR CANDY and KIN.

the gift that keeps on living...

blanky

kealan patrick burke

Made in the USA
Middletown, DE
21 July 2018